The Very Hungry
Lions

A STORY OF DANIEL

John Ryan

A LION PICTURE STORY

"There are many stories about your famous cousin Daniel," said Granny Leah, as the children gathered round for their bedtime story. "Tonight I'm going to tell you one from long, long ago...

"I was just a little girl at the time. We Jewish people were captives in the city of Babylon because our enemies had conquered our own lands.

"Babylon was one of the greatest cities in the world, with wonderful gardens and a wide river running through it. The people of Babylon loved lions. They had pictures and carvings of lions all over their gates and palaces.

"They even kept a den of fierce hungry lions—just to eat up the very worst criminals!

"Belshazzar, the King of Babylon, was really wicked. He worshipped false idols and, of course, thought nothing of our God, the true God of Israel. My father–your great-grandfather–was a wine steward at the court, so he knew all about Belshazzar and his evil ways.

"One night, the king gave a great feast for all his courtiers and friends.

"It was so noisy!
I couldn't sleep a wink,
even though my little
room was at the far
end of the palace.

"So, in the end,
I slipped out of bed...

"...and crept along the huge corridors.

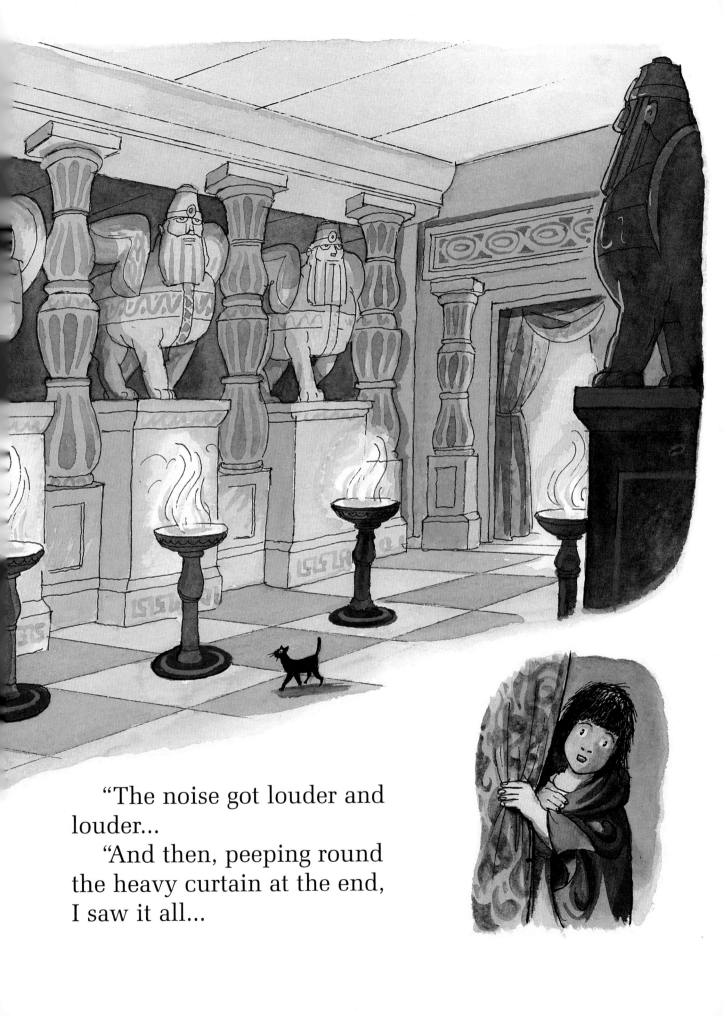

"The noise got louder and
louder...
"And then, peeping round
the heavy curtain at the end,
I saw it all...

"There were
people eating and drinking
and shouting and dancing. I could see my
father filling Belshazzar's golden cup with wine.

"Then, suddenly,
everything went quiet.
I saw the king
staring wide-eyed at
the wall high above
him. He turned pale,
dropped his cup,
and pointed...

"There was a hand in the air, writing strange words high up on the wall opposite. Everyone watched, dumbstruck!

"'What means this?' cried the terrified King Belshazzar.

"But nobody there could help him. Try as they might, even his wisest advisers couldn't tell him what the mysterious writing meant.

"Then, after a while, I saw Daniel arrive. He was already famous among our people because of his strength and honesty and wisdom, but I was surprised to see him there.

"Daniel looked at those strange words and spoke solemnly to the king. At this, King Belshazzar seemed more terrified than ever. Then, suddenly, there came a fearful shouting and fierce war cries.

"Armed men rushed into the hall!

"The lamps were thrown over!
The guests shrieked in terror!

"And I ran for my life... back to my bed,
and hid under my blanket.

"The next morning I thought it had all been a bad dream. But my father told me it was true.

"'King Belshazzar is dead,' he said. 'God warned him about his wicked ways in strange words written on the wall. But it was too late. Last night he was killed by our new king—Darius."

"Soon after that, my father gave up being a wine steward. 'It's far too dangerous!' he said. He got a new job—looking after the king's lions. You might think that was dangerous too, but my father always was good with animals.

"Meanwhile, Daniel had become one of the new king's most trusted friends and advisers...

"...so much so that the other important people at the royal court became very jealous of him.

"Darius was quite a good king, but he had some strange ideas. He thought he was so great and grand and important that he was almost a god!

"So Daniel's enemies pretended to agree with him. 'Great King,' they said, 'make a law that anybody who prays to any god other than you will be thrown into the lions' den.'

"Darius was fooled by their flattery and he agreed to the new law. He didn't realize that his friend Daniel could never obey it, for Daniel always prayed to the one true God of Israel and to no other.

"So it was that the wicked advisers were able to come to Darius and say, 'Look, O King, your false friend Daniel is not praying to you. He prays to another god. Surely he must be thrown to the lions!'

"Too late, King Darius saw how he had been tricked. He knew that any law that he made *had* to be obeyed, and he tried to persuade his friend to change his mind.

"But Daniel refused to obey the new law, so he was handed over to the guards, who took him to the lions' den.

"King Darius watched as my father pushed Daniel into the den, and sealed the entrance. 'Sorry, Daniel,' he said, 'but orders are orders.'

"He was surprised to see how calm Daniel looked. He didn't seem worried about being thrown to those terrible wild beasts.

"We heard afterwards that King Darius had a very bad night. They brought him delicious food and drink, and musicians came to play him to sleep, but he sent them all away.

"He lay there tossing and turning, wondering what had happened to his friend Daniel.
"Next morning he got up very early...

"threw on some clothes...

"... and
hurried to the lions' den.

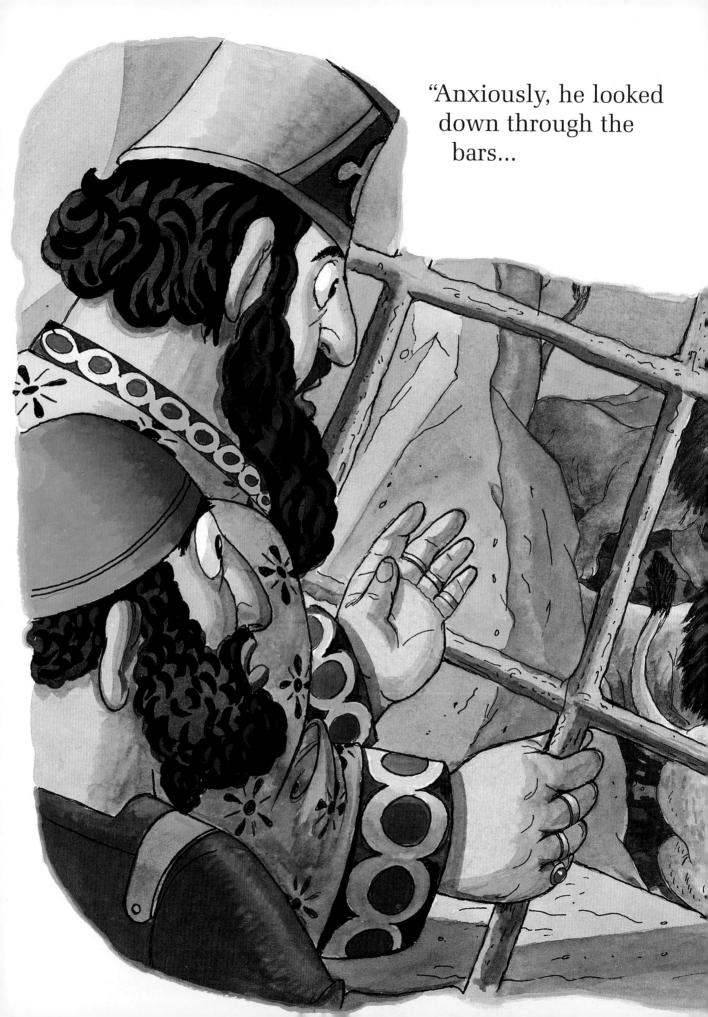

"Anxiously, he looked down through the bars...

" 'Oh Daniel, what have I done?' he cried, hardly expecting an answer.

"But to his surprise he heard a voice: 'I am alive and well, O King.' It was Daniel! He was standing there quite unhurt, with the lions all around him.

"All this time my father had been watching in amazement. He opened the entrance and helped Daniel out of the den.

"'How did you escape the jaws of those terrible beasts?' asked the king.

"'Did that God of yours rescue you?'

"'He did, indeed,' said Daniel. 'He heard my prayers and sent his angel to tame the lions. The angel told them not to hurt me, so we all spent a peaceful night together.'

"At last, King Darius saw how foolish he had been to think of himself as a god. So he made another law, a good one this time, to say that everybody in his kingdom should worship only Daniel's God. For Daniel had been right all along.

"He continued to be the king's friend, and he went on to become even more important and powerful.

"And that," said Granny Leah, "is the end of this story."
"But, Granny," asked the children. "What happened to the king's wicked advisers, the people who plotted to send Daniel to the lions' den?"
"Something very terrible, I'm sure..." said Granny Leah. "But now it's time you were off to bed."

"And don't forget to say your prayers...

"...just like Daniel."

The author asserts the moral right
to be identified as the author of this work

Published by
Lion Publishing plc
Sandy Lane West, Oxford, England
ISBN 0 7459 3601 6
Lion Publishing
4050 Lee Vance View, Colorado Springs,
CO 80918, USA
ISBN 0 7459 3723 3
Albatross Books Pty Ltd
PO Box 320, Sutherland,
NSW 2232, Australia
ISBN 0 7324 1458 X

First edition 1996
10 9 8 7 6 5 4 3 2 1 0

A catalogue record for this book is available
from the British Library

Printed and bound in Malaysia